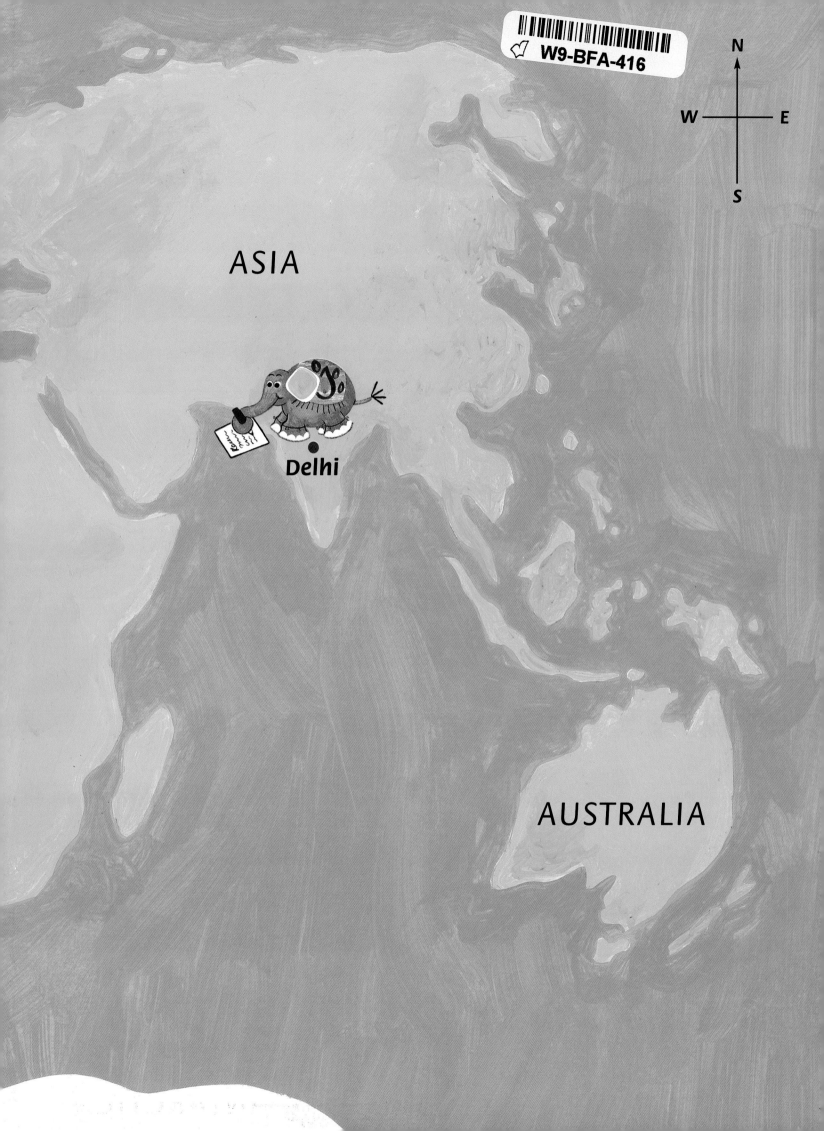

Published in 2002 by Sterling Publishing Co., Inc.
387 Park Avenue South, New York, NY 10016

First published in Great Britain in 2001 by Brimax
an imprint of Octopus Publishing Group Ltd
2-4 Heron Quays, London E14 4JP
© Octopus Publishing Group Ltd

Library of Congress Cataloging-in-Publication Data Available

10 9 8 7 6 5 4 3 2 1

Distributed in Canada by Sterling Publishing Co., Inc.

C/o Canadian Manda Group,
One Atlantic Avenue, Suite 105
Toronto, Ontario, Canada M6K 3E7

Sterling ISBN 0-8069-7837-6

Lost Little Elephant

Alison Morris • Olivia Rayner

Sterling Publishing Co., Inc.
New York

Little Elephant lived on the Cape of Good Hope, in Africa.
Even though he was called "Little," he had huge, flappy ears,
just like all African elephants. One day, Little Elephant
received a letter from his Indian cousin, Aziz.

Legend has it that the waters around the Cape of Good Hope are haunted by a ghost ship called the Flying Dutchman.

Dear Cousin,

Next month there is going to be a very big carnival here in Delhi.
The streets will be lined with flowers, and all the buildings will be covered with flags.
There will be cake for everyone. Would you like to visit?

With lots of love,
Aziz

As he read the letter, Little Elephant grew more and more excited. "I'm on my way!" he laughed. That very day, Little Elephant set out on his long, long journey to India.

Although Little Elephant had never been to India before,
he was sure he could find his way.
His ancestors had made the long trip
thousands of years ago. As everyone knows,
an elephant never forgets!

South Africa is home to the
world's tallest animal, the giraffe;
the smallest, the pygmy shrew;
and the fastest, the cheetah!

Little Elephant headed north. Soon he was hot and thirsty, but there was no shelter from the hot sun, and nothing to drink but dry mud! But on and on he marched.

He came to Cape Town, a huge city where there were lots of people and buildings. Little Elephant saw a mountain with the top chopped off, and cable cars going up the side.

Table Mountain is home to a hooved mammal called a rock hyrax. Although it is only rabbit-sized, this creature's closest living relative is the ELEPHANT!

People were sitting beside a marina. But there were no flags to be seen, and hardly any cake.

After Little Elephant had rested awhile, drunk all the water from the marina...

and eaten all the amaryllis plants (which made his tummy feel a bit full)...

he decided to keep marching north.

For many days, Little Elephant marched on, until he reached the city of Cairo. It was very different to the last city. Some buildings were new and some were ancient.

Ancient Egyptians, believed they would need their food, money, and pets in the afterlife.

After Little Elephant had rested awhile, drunk the Nile dry...

But instead of flags, flowers, and cake, he saw pyramids with strange statues guarding them, and an enormous museum.

The Great Pyramids were huge burial tombs. Built on the west bank of the River Nile, they are the last surviving wonder of the ancient world.

Guarding the Pyramids, the Sphinx is half-man and half-lion.

and eaten most of the valley's date trees...

he decided to keep walking.

But Little Elephant had traveled too far to give up. "Ship ahoy!" he called, and squished himself onto a tiny fishing boat going further north. Using his long trunk, Little Elephant helped the fisherman pull in his catch.

At last, land got closer
and closer, until... BUMP!
Little Elephant landed.

The Vatican is a city within a city! Although its walls are inside Rome, it was given to the Catholic Church in 1929, and now has its own laws, money, and even postage stamps!

Wobbling around on his land legs, Little Elephant thought, "Surely I must be in Delhi now!" But instead of flags, flowers, and cake, he saw a small city within a city! He was in Rome!

The Colosseum was built by the Romans, long before Rome was part of Italy. This is where the gladiators fought each other in front of thuge crowds.

So after Little Elephant had rested awhile, drunk the Trevi Fountain dry...

and eaten all the pizza in the city...

There were lots of little motorcycles called scooters whizzing around. Above it all towered an old colosseum that looked like it might topple down!

he decided to keep traveling— in local style!

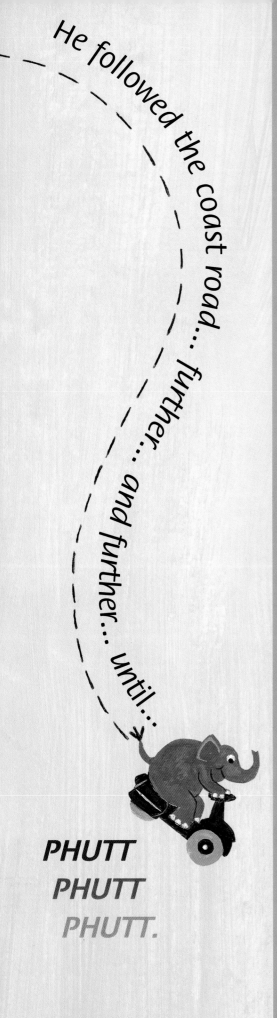

He followed the coast road... further... and further... until...

PHUTT
PHUTT
PHUTT.

He ran out of gas! Where was Little Elephant now?

He was lost in Barcelona! But Little Elephant didn't mind. There was so much to see.

The Sagrada Familia Cathedral was designed by a famous Spanish architect named Antoni Gaudi. They started building it in 1882, and it still isn't finished!

There was a big cathedral with spires and arches, and the streets were full of dancers, musicians, and acrobats. It was a magical city, but it was not Delhi.

Barcelona's La Ramblas is the most famous walkway in Spain, but it was once only a ravine to carry rainwater to the sea!

So after Little Elephant had rested awhile, drunk the harbor dry...

and eaten all the paella in the city...

he decided to continue by train.

The Arc de Triomphe was built for Napoleon Bonaparte to celebrate his military victories.

The train chugged through mountains and thick forests, over rolling hills and green meadows until finally it stopped. But just where was Little Elephant now?

He was so excited to see Paris that he forgot to look for flags and flowers, although his tummy was rumbling for cake.

When the Eiffel Tower was built in 1889, it was the world's tallest building.

The food in Paris is among the best in the world.

Little Elephant saw a great arch proudly standing in the center, an iron tower reaching up into the clouds, and artists painting on every avenue.

So after Little Elephant had rested awhile, drunk the River Seine dry...

and eaten all the bread and cheese in the city...

he pedaled back to the train station.

Nelson's Column, which is over 160 feet tall, was built to honor Lord Nelson's victory at the Battle of Trafalgar. The lions at the bottom are made from captured French cannons.

This time when Little Elephant stepped off the train, he saw more water falling from the sky than even he could fit into his great big belly! Where could he be? He saw lots of things to give him clues.

So after Little Elephant had rested awhile, drunk the Thames dry...

Big Ben is the nickname for the clock tower attached to the Houses of Parliament.

The soldiers who guard Buckingham Palace are not allowed to speak to anyone, or even smile!

There was a very tall statue guarded by lions, and lots of soldiers in red coats and furry black hats guarding a palace. He was in London!

and eaten all the fish and chips in the city, he climbed onto a bus...

to see where it would take him. The last stop was the airport.

Icebergs can rise up to over 300 feet above the waterline—only a tiny bit of their actual size!

You can take a lovely warm bath in the hot springs in Greenland.

Little Elephant decided to fly as far north as he could go. But he soon started to feel cold, which was something he had never felt before! All that Little Elephant could see below was snow and ice.

During the Arctic summer, the sun never sets! At all other times, there is hardly any light at all.

How different this looked to an elephant used to warm grasslands! Once Little Elephant reached chilly Greenland, he flew on in search of a warmer place. He decided to leap out at the first city he came to!

Toronto has the world's largest underground shopping mall. It's very cold in winter, so people often travel underground.

As Little Elephant parachuted down, he looked at the amazing city! He saw a huge tower shooting up into the sky like a rocket, and a city hall that looked as if it had landed from outer space!

Standing 1,815 feet high, the CN Tower is the world's tallest building. You can eat at the restaurant at 1,150 feet!

Little Elephant saw some wonderful things in Toronto, but he still hadn't found Delhi.

So after he had rested awhile, drunk Lake Ontario dry...

and eaten at all the restaurants in the city...

Little Elephant decided to travel south.

Niagara Falls forms a natural border between Canada and the USA.

The Empire State Building is so tall that it has been struck by lightning! On a clear day, visitors can see for 80 miles.

SOUTH

NORTH

shops

BiG SHOP

On his way south, Little Elephant stopped to have a dip and a drink in a huge waterfall.

A statue of a very large woman was holding a torch to light up the harbor. There were so many tall buildings, and so many shops to see!

New York is famous for its skyscrapers, tall offices, and apartment buildings that reach for the sky!

The Statue of Liberty is a symbol of peace and democracy.

New York was full of museums and Broadway shows. But Little Elephant still needed to get to Delhi.

After Little Elephant had rested awhile, drunk most of the Hudson River...

and eaten every single hotdog in town...

he got into a yellow cab and headed south.

Dallas, Texas, is a bustling city with huge skyscrapers and museums. But it is still very attached to its wild West past. Even its football team is called The Cowboys!

Elvis Presley was a famous rock 'n' roll star. His home, Graceland, in Memphis, Tennessee, is the second most visited house in the United States.

Elvis Presley in Memphis...

and a Dallas sheriff, before going on his way.

The Angel of Independence represents Mexico's fight for independence from Spain. At its base are four statues, symbolizing War, Peace, Justice, and Law.

The further south Little Elephant went, the warmer the weather became. Soon, it was so hot that it felt almost like home. But he was still very far from home!

Little Elephant had never seen so many people in one place! Guarding over Mexico City was a statue of a beautiful angel.

More than 20 million people live in Mexico City—that's almost a quarter of the country's entire population!

So after Little Elephant had rested awhile, drunk every bottle of water in the city...

and eaten all the chilli he could find...

he continued on his way south.

There were even remains from an ancient Aztec city. But there were no flags, flowers, or cake.

The Angel Falls in Venezuela are the highest waterfalls in the world!

On and on he went... through waterfalls... past the jungle... over hills and

The Uros people of Bolivia live on rafts on the lake, in small floating villages.

dressed local people ...and on... and on through thick jungle... until finally he could see, in the distance, the sea... and boarded

Machu Picchu in Peru is the remains of an ancient Inca city. The Incas had a mighty empire from AD 1438 until they were beaten by Spanish invaders in 1532.

mountains covered in more jungle... past ancient cities... in the jungle... past beautiful sandy beaches...

Christ the Redeemer statue in Brazil stands at a height of 2,329 feet high above the city of Rio de Janeiro.

past more jungle... past brightly

Iguacu are massive waterfalls stretching over a mile long. Cutting through the rainforest, they form a natural border between Brazil, Argentina, and Paraguay.

another ship. The rolling waves rocked Little Elephant to sleep!

Sydney Opera House is famous for its unusual design. Built between 1958 and 1973, some people think it looks like a ship, but its design was actually based on segments of an orange!

Little Elephant awoke to find himself sailing into a big, beautiful harbor. There was a building with lots of arched roofs that looked like a huge sailing ship, and a very long bridge that went from one end of the harbor to the other.

Sydney Harbour Bridge is the heaviest steel bridge in the world – it weighs an amazing 52,800 tons!

The busy Sydney harbor was crowded with yachts and sailing ships of all sizes. But there were no flags, flowers, or cake.

So after Little Elephant had rested awhile, drunk the harbor dry...

and eaten every single sausage off every single barbecue...

he got on a surfboard, and off he went. Time to go north again!

Little Elephant completed the longest surf in elephant history, and then took a stroll around Bangkok, where there were huge gold statues and even bigger golden temples.

Inside The Temple of Wat Phra Kaeo, the Emerald Buddha sits on top of a high gilded altar.

So after Little Elephant had rested awhile, drunk the Chao Phraya River dry...

Some people walked around with all their belongings strapped to their backs, while others sold their goods from boats on the river.

Bangkok, or Krung Thep, means the City of Angels.

and eaten all the durian fruit in the floating market...

tuk tuk tuk tuk tuk tuk tuk tuk

he climbed into a local taxi, and wondered where he'd end up next.

At last Little Elephant reached a city decorated with flags.
There were plates of cakes everywhere. But was it Delhi?
He explored the city's temples and a big fort.

The Red Fort, or Lal Quila, is one of the largest monuments in Delhi.

The festival of Ganesh Chaturthi celebrates the birth of Lord Ganesh, a Hindu god with an elephant's head.

All around were statues with elephants' heads draped in flowers. Then, across the crowds, who did Little Elephant see... his cousin Aziz! Little Elephant was finally in Delhi!

Little Elephant and Aziz danced the night away on the streets of Delhi and ate all the cake they could see. Little Elephant told his cousin about the wonderful places he had seen. "But next time," he said with a smile, "you must come and visit me!"

Guidance Notes

This book has been specially designed to help children learn about geography in an entertaining way. Little Elephant's adventure takes in famous cities, amazing monuments, foreign cultures, exotic climates, and the natural wonders of the world.

In order for children to get the most from this book, the following pages provide some fun activities to share together.

- Go back through the book to discover where Little Elephant saw certain sights. Children will enjoy studying the illustrations to find the answers.

- There are also some suggested questions to ask about Little Elephant's travels.

- At the end of the book, you will find a map on which you can trace Little Elephant's journey.

- Why not ask which city your child would most like to visit?

- Discuss which route to India might have been quicker for Little Elephant.

Little Elephant saw many amazing sights on his journey. Can you remember where he saw the things below?

Little Elephant traveled to many different countries and cities. How well do you remember his trip?

1. Where is the Sphinx?

2. Where did Little Elephant have his picture painted?

3. What did Little Elephant eat in Rome, Italy?

4. Where does the President of the USA live?

5. How much does Sydney Harbor Bridge weigh?

6. What is the mountain in Cape Town, South Africa called?

7. What is the world's tallest building?

8. Where did Little Elephant eat fish and chips?

9. What does the name Bangkok mean?

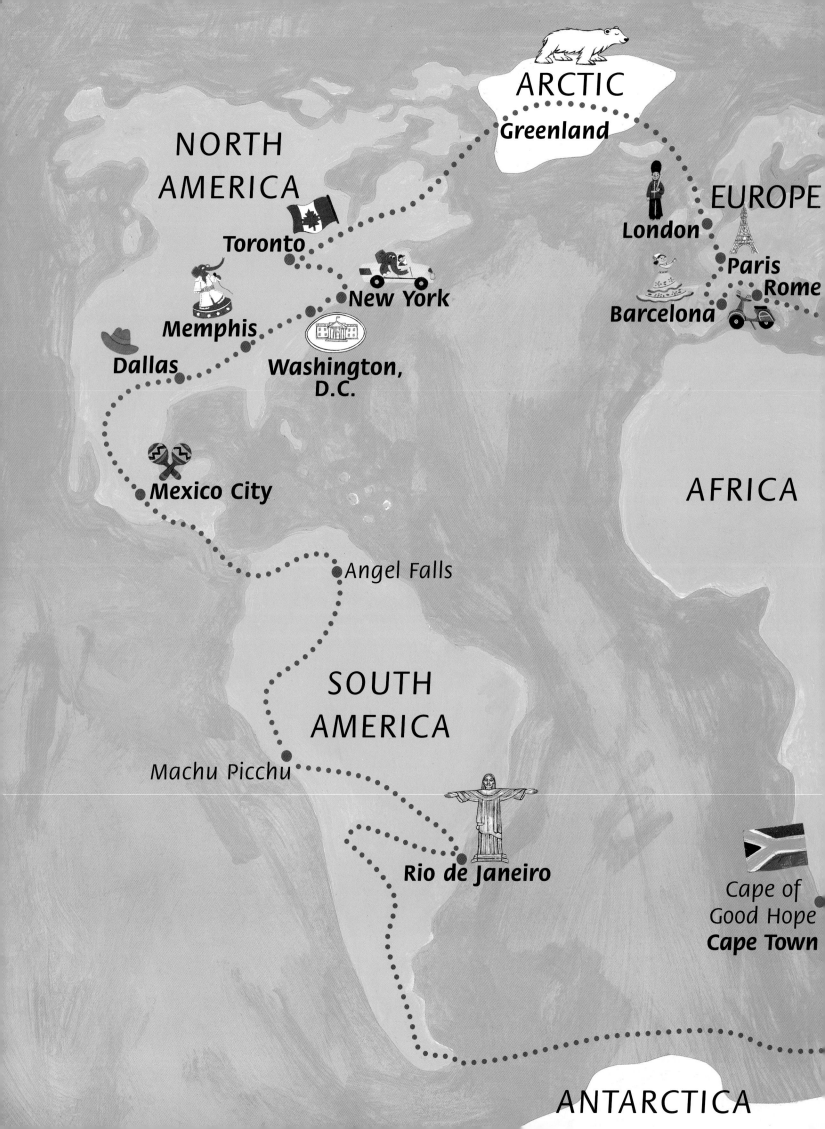